Eagle-Eye Ernie Comes to Town

Eagle-Eye Ernie
Comes to Town

by Susan Pearson
illustrated by Gioia Fiammenghi

SIMON AND SCHUSTER BOOKS FOR YOUNG READERS
PUBLISHED BY SIMON & SCHUSTER INC.
New York • London • Toronto • Sydney • Tokyo • Singapore

SIMON AND SCHUSTER BOOKS FOR YOUNG READERS

Simon & Schuster Building, Rockefeller Center, 1230 Avenue of the Americas, New York, New York 10020. Text copyright © 1990 by Susan Pearson. Illustrations copyright © 1990 by Gioia Fiammenghi. All rights reserved including the right of reproduction in whole or in part in any form. SIMON AND SCHUSTER BOOKS FOR YOUNG READERS is a trademark of Simon & Schuster Inc. Designed by Lucille Chomowicz   Manufactured in the United States of America
10 9 8 7 6 5 4 3 2 1   pbk. 10 9 8 7 6 5 4 3 2
Library of Congress Cataloging-in-Publication Data. Pearson, Susan. Eagle-Eye Ernie comes to town. Summary: A new kid in school named Ernie solves the case of the lunch bag thief using her powers of deduction and her "eagle eye."   [1. Mystery and detective stories.   2. Schools— Fiction.]   I. Fiammenghi, Gioia, ill.   II. Title. PZ7.P323316Eag   1990   [Fic]—dc20 89-26210   ISBN 0-671-70564-4   ISBN 0-671-70568-7 (pbk.)

For David Bailey,
who introduced me to Ernie — SP

To Laura — GF

CONTENTS

CHAPTER 1

No Bear Lake

Ernestine Jones was mad. Her daddy had made a big mistake.

"You'll love Minnesota," he had told her. Well, he was wrong!

Ernie slammed the back door. She dropped her backpack loudly onto the kitchen counter. The noise sounded good.

She marched to the refrigerator. She

pulled the door open. She grabbed an apple. She slammed the door.

Crunch. She took a bite. *Chomp, chomp, chomp.* She chewed as loudly as she could.

"Hello, lamb," said Mommy from the doorway. Her hair was tied up in a scarf. She had a smudge of dirt on her nose. She had been unpacking boxes.

"Don't call me that!" said Ernie.

"Bad day?" asked Mommy.

"I hate school," said Ernie. "I hate Minnesota!" She sat down hard on a kitchen chair.

Mommy sat down, too. "What don't you like?" she asked. "Your teacher?"

"Ms. Finney is all right," said Ernie. "It's the kids. They said I talk funny. They said Virginia must be on Mars. They said only Martians wear saddle shoes."

Ernie started to cry. She kicked her saddle shoes against the chair legs.

"I hate saddle shoes!" She cried harder.

"Come here, babe," said Mommy. She patted her lap. Ernie climbed into it. Pretty soon she wouldn't fit anymore. She was glad pretty soon wasn't yet.

Mommy hugged her. "The first day in a new school is hard," she said. "But it will get better, Ernie. I promise."

"Can I wear sneakers to school tomorrow?" Ernie asked.

"No," said Mommy. "Sneakers are bad for your arches."

"Who cares about stupid arches, anyway?"

"I do," said Mommy. "Come on." She lifted Ernie off her lap. "I have a surprise for you. Your bedroom is all unpacked."

Ernie followed Mommy to her new bedroom. Except for two boxes in the middle of the floor, everything was in its place. Her brand-new dinosaur poster hung over her bed. Her friendly old Cookie Monster poster hung beside it. Her Frog and Toad poster hung over her bookcase. Her shell wind chimes that she had made herself hung by the window. A map of the United States hung over her desk.

"I left those boxes for you," said Mommy. "I thought you would like to unpack them yourself."

Ernie wiped her eyes on her sleeve. These were the best boxes. She knew exactly what was inside them. It was all her best stuff. She was glad Mommy had not unpacked them.

Ernie got right to work. She put Ellie and Teddy and Dina on her bed. She put Pie Face and Moby Duck on her chest.

She set up her milk carton village on top of her bookcase. She put Mr. Frog next to the library. He was the librarian. She put Miss Mouse in front of Town Hall. She was the mayor.

Harold was at the bottom of the second box. Ernie set him gently on her desk. Then she sat down. She petted Harold's back. The paint had made it smooth. He didn't feel like a rock anymore. He didn't feel like a turtle either, really. He just felt like Harold.

Ernie stared at the map over her desk. A wide blue line traced over the roads from Newport News, Virginia to White Bear Lake, Minnesota. Daddy had helped her draw it.

White Bear Lake. What a stupid name for a town. There weren't any white bears here. There weren't any bears at all.

White Bear Lake was so stupid, it wasn't even on the map. They had to write it in. Newport News was on the map, though. So there!

Ernie opened her desk drawer. She took out her ruler. She measured between Newport News and stupid No Bear Lake. Sixteen inches. Was that all? Sixty million miles. That's how far it felt.

Ernie stared at the wide blue line. It zig-zagged across Virginia. It bent up through Kentucky. It cut off the bottoms of Indiana and Illinois. It cut Missouri in half. Then it marched straight up through Iowa to No Bear Lake, Minnesota.

Suddenly, she had an idea.

"Mommy!" Ernie yelled. She ran to the living room. Mommy was hanging pictures. "Where is the shoe polish?"

"In the shoe box under the sink," said Mommy. "Going to polish your shoes?"

"I'm going to fix them," said Ernie.

"Want some help?" asked Mommy.

"Nope," said Ernie.

"Here," said Mommy. She handed Ernie some old newspapers. "Spread these out under you. I don't want shoe polish spilled on my new floor."

"I'll be careful," Ernie promised.

She skipped to the kitchen. She spread the

newspapers on the floor. She got the shoe box from under the sink. There was black shoe polish. There was blue shoe polish. And there was red shoe polish. Good, good, good.

Ernie took off her shoes. She opened the black bottle first. She sang,

"The bears went over the mountain,
The bears went over the mountain . . ."

She painted a big black nose on the toe of each shoe. Next she opened the blue bottle.

"The bears went over the mountain,
To see what they could see."

She painted two blue eyes above the noses.
Finally, she opened the red shoe polish. She painted a little bear mouth below each nose.

Ernie looked at her work. Something was

wrong. Ears! Of course! Bears needed ears.

Ernie skipped to her bedroom. She opened her desk drawer. She took out the glue.

She skipped to the bathroom. She looked under the sink. Sure enough, there was the bag of cotton balls. She took four. Then she took two more.

She skipped back into the kitchen. She sang,

"The bears went over the mountain,
The bears went over the mountain,
The bears went over the mountain,
To hear what they could hear."

Ernie glued two cotton ears onto each toe. She glued a cotton tail onto each heel. Then she looked at her work again. Perfect! Now No Bear Lake had two white bears.

She could hardly wait to wear her bears to school tomorrow.

CHAPTER 2

Two White Bears

Ernie was on her way to school.

"The bears hopped over the sidewalk," she sang.

Step-step-step-hop, she walked.

"The bears hopped over the sidewalk . . ."

Step-step-step-hop.

Her bears' ears bounced with every hop. Ernie couldn't see her heels, but she was sure their tails were bouncing, too.

"The bears hopped over the sidewalk,
   On their way to school." *Hop!*
Ernie step-hopped over to the jungle gym.
Four of the kids in her new class were on it.

A girl named Marcie was sitting in the crow's nest. She had yellow hair and she smelled like Juicy Fruit gum—sweet and sticky. Ernie sat right behind her in Ms. Finney's room. It took all morning for the smell to go away. After lunch, the smell was back again. Ernie didn't like it.

A boy named William was hanging from the ladder. Ernie sat right next to him. He was skinny and he didn't talk much. Ernie guessed he drew better than he talked or ate. Yesterday she had watched him drawing all during arithmetic.

Another girl named Rachel was climbing up the slide. She had the fattest braids Ernie had ever seen. Maybe they were a wig. Ernie wished she could pull one to find out.

A boy named Michael was hanging by his knees. He was wearing big headphones. They weren't connected to anything.

"Hey," Ernie called to him.

"Hey, what?" Michael called back.

"What do you mean, 'Hey, what'?" said Ernie. "Just 'Hey.'"

"That's Martian talk," said Michael. "You're a Martian girl." And he began to sing,

> "Ernie is a Martian,
> Ernie is a Martian."

"She is not," said Rachel. "My mother told me so. She just has a Southern accent."

Marcie smiled a sweet, sticky smile. It wasn't a friendly smile. "She is too," she said. "She's a Martian queen. Ernestine is a Martian queen."

Soon the whole jungle gym was singing it.

> "Er-ness-*teen* is a Martian *queen*!
> Er-ness-*teen* is a Martian *queen*!"

12

Ernie felt her face getting hot. Her eyes burned. Her hands turned into fists. Her tummy flip-flopped.

Just then Rachel came down the slide. She walked right up to Ernie.

"My name is Rachel," she said. "You can call me R.T."

"I'm Ernie," said Ernie. "Why is he wearing those headphones?"

"He is listening to Mission Control," said R.T. "He hangs by his knees like that to practice being weightless. Come on. I'll show you something really neat."

Ernie followed her around the corner of the school.

"Shhh," said R.T. She crept up under one of the windows.

Ernie followed. They peeked inside.

Mr. Conway, the assistant principal, sat at his desk. He talked on the telephone. He wrote something down on a piece of paper.

Ernie didn't see anything neat.

"Just wait," R.T. whispered.

Ernie waited. Nothing neat happened. She waited some more. Still nothing.

"Shoot," said R.T. She backed away from the window. Ernie followed.

"He doesn't do it every day," said R.T.

"What does he do?" Ernie asked.

"Some days he picks his nose," R.T. told her. "It's really neat."

Just then the bell rang. Ernie and R.T. ran for the door.

The morning dragged by. Reading. Spelling. Arithmetic. Nature.

Ernie sat very still in her seat. She hoped Ms. Finney didn't see quiet children. She didn't want to be called on. She didn't want to talk. If she didn't talk, maybe no one would laugh at her.

She stared at the clock. It was almost time for lunch.

"Ernie?" said Ms. Finney.

Rats! thought Ernie.

"Yes, ma'am," she said.

Michael giggled.

"That's enough, Michael," said Ms. Finney. "And take those headphones off, please."

She pulled down a map of the United States. "Ernie, will you come to the front and show us where you went to school last year."

Ernie marched to the front of the room. She took the pointer from Ms. Finney. She pointed to Newport News, Virginia.

Michael began to giggle again. At first it was just a little chuckle. But it grew. Soon the whole class was laughing.

Ernie didn't get it. What was so funny about an old map, anyway? She looked at Ms. Finney. Ms. Finney didn't get it, either.

They both looked at Michael. By now he

was laughing too hard to tell them what was so funny, but Marcie wasn't. She smiled her sweet, sticky smile.

"Look at her feet, Ms. Finney," she said.

Ernie looked down at her shoes. She had forgotten all about her white bears.

Ms. Finney looked down at Ernie's shoes. She started to smile. Ernie was afraid she was going to laugh, too. But she didn't.

"They're Martian shoes!" shouted Michael.

The class laughed harder.

Ms. Finney rapped on her desk. *"Quiet!"* she said. She looked right at Michael. Her face was angry.

Then she looked at Ernie. She smiled. "Would you like to tell us about your shoes, Ernie?" she asked.

But Ernie didn't get a chance. Instead, the lunch bell rang.

Ernie got in line with the hot lunch kids.

The baggers got their lunch bags. Then they got in line, too.

The kids who walked home for lunch put on their jackets. They walked quietly to the door. Then they raced out into the September sun. Ernie wished she was a walker.

CHAPTER 3

The Lunch Bag Thief

Ernie went through the lunch line. Macaroni mess and canned peas. Yuck. Tomorrow she'd bring her lunch. Or better yet, she'd go home for lunch.

She carried her tray to Room 123's table.

R.T. waved to her. "Sit here, Ernie," she called. She pointed to the empty seat beside her. "I have a bunny at home," said R.T. "His name is Ralph. He looks like your shoes."

"They're not bunnies," Ernie told her. "They're bears. White bears. For White Bear Lake."

"Wow," said R.T., "that's neat! Maybe I could make my shoes into tigers. We could start a shoe zoo."

Ernie felt warm all over. Maybe this would be a good day after all.

Suddenly, Michael jumped up. "Who took my Twinkie?" he yelled. "I always get a Twinkie in my lunch."

Then Marcie stood up. "My sandwich is missing!" she cried.

R.T. opened her bag. "My carrots are gone!"

"And my pickle," whispered Jason. Jason always whispered. Ernie guessed he was shy. He wiped his nose on his sleeve. He did that a lot, too.

R.T. twisted one of her braids around her finger. Then she began to chew on it. It didn't come off, but Ernie still wanted to pull it, just to make sure.

"It must be Dinosaur Don," said R.T.

"Who is Dinosaur Don?" Ernie asked.

"The fat fifth-grader over there," said R.T. She pointed to the fifth-grade table. "He's a giant bully."

"He kicked my dog *twice*," whispered Jason.

"Last year he stole my milk money," said Sammy. "Every day for two months."

"What made him stop?" asked Ernie.

"School ended," said Sammy.

"It must be him, then," said Ernie.

"Nah," said Michael. "Dino Don would take the whole lunch."

"Or just the desserts," said Sammy. His glasses were slipping. He pushed them back up his nose. "He wouldn't take a pickle. Or carrots, either."

The table got very noisy. Everyone was shouting. Ernie couldn't tell what they were saying.

Michael shouted something to Sammy.

Then Sammy shouted to Marcie.

Then Marcie shouted to Jason.

Suddenly, it got very quiet. Everyone, even R.T., stared at Ernie.

"What are you looking at me for?" said Ernie.

Marcie smiled her sweet, sticky smile. "This never happened before you came," she said.

Ernie felt her face get hot for the second time that day.

"I didn't take your stuff!" she told them. "Look!" She pointed at her tray.

"You ate it already," said Michael. "Martians eat all day long."

All afternoon the whole room whispered

about the lunch bag thief. Nobody whispered to Ernie, but she could hear them. And every time she looked up, someone was staring at her.

Ernie felt itchy all over. She wanted to wiggle. She wanted to scratch. But she didn't do it. If she moved, they would all stare harder at her, so she sat still. She stared straight ahead at Marcie's yellow hair. She hated yellow hair.

For art that day, they painted.

Michael painted a picture of a Martian. He was green. He had two heads and six arms. He had four feet. On each foot there was a white bear shoe.

Marcie painted a picture of a yellow-haired girl. She wore a frilly dress. She had flowers in her hair. She had a sweet, sticky smile. If pictures smelled, she would smell like Juicy Fruit gum. Ernie was sure of it.

William painted a picture of a rabbit. It

was really good. Ernie wanted to touch it. It looked so soft.

Ernie painted a picture of a big white bear. It looked angry and sad at the same time. Just like she felt.

She took her paintbrush to the sink.

Marcie and Michael were already there. Marcie was whispering to Michael. When Ernie came up, she stopped.

Even R.T. didn't talk to her. There would be no shoe zoo now.

Finally, the bell rang. Ernie was the first one out the classroom door. She broke a school rule and ran down the hall. She ran across the playground. She ran all the way home. Her bears' ears bounced all the way, but Ernie didn't care.

CHAPTER 4

The Eagle Eye

"It's all your fault," Ernie told Daddy that night. "You should have kept your old job."

"Whoa," said Daddy. "What's all this about?"

Ernie told him every terrible thing about her terrible day.

"Hmmm," said Daddy. "Well, I think I can straighten some things out."

"Are you going to catch the lunch bag thief?" Ernie asked.

"Not that, I'm afraid," said Daddy.

"Then what?" said Ernie.

"For one thing," said Daddy, "people don't say 'hey' in Minnesota. They say 'hi.' Michael didn't know what you meant."

"Oh," said Ernie. She didn't like Michael one bit better.

"And another thing," said Daddy, "people up north don't say 'ma'am' and 'sir,' either."

"People up north are rude," said Ernie. "We should go home."

Daddy laughed. "They're not rude, Ernie," he said. "They just have different ways."

"What about the lunch bag thief?" said Ernie. "He is rude."

"Yes," Daddy agreed. "He is rude."

"Everyone thinks he is me," said Ernie.

"But we know better than that," said Daddy.

"I want them to know better than that, too," said Ernie.

"Then I guess you'll have to find the thief," said Daddy.

"I can't do that!" said Ernie.

"Why not?" said Daddy. "You are the best finder I know."

This was true. Whenever Daddy lost his glasses, Ernie found them. Whenever Mommy lost an earring, Ernie found it. Ernie had an eagle eye.

Just wait! If that thief did it again, Ernie would find him. First she would shake him. Then she would take him straight to Mr. Conway's office. Mr. Conway would be so surprised! He might even pick his nose for her.

*   *   *

Sure enough, things were missing from lunch bags again on Wednesday.

Ellen's sandwich was gone. "All I have now is an apple," she said. She looked like she might cry. "I hate apples!"

"I'll eat it," said Tommy. "My doughnut is gone." He was so mad, his face was all red.

Sammy's orange was missing, too. He was the only one who didn't mind. "The juice always sprays on my glasses," he explained.

Ernie had brought her lunch from home today, too. Nothing was missing from it. Nothing was missing from R.T.'s lunch, either. Or from Marcie's. Or from Jason's. But Michael's Twinkie was gone again.

Serves him right, Ernie thought.

Ernie ate fast. It was important to get to work right away.

She took her empty bag to the trash can. She dropped it in. Then she hid behind a door.

She kept one eagle eye on the trash can.

She kept the other out for Dinosaur Don.

This school sure made a lot of garbage—milk cartons, dirty napkins, cold green beans, sloppy-joe gunk. But no Twinkies wrapper. No orange peel.

Finally, Dinosaur Don came to the window. He didn't make any garbage at all. He dropped his fork into the dishpan. He dropped his tray onto the belt. They both looked like he had licked them clean.

Ernie sighed. Dinosaur Don was her best suspect. But if he wasn't it, then who was?

Suddenly, Ernie had a thought. What if the thief was a bagger? Then the evidence would be hidden inside a bag. She would have to go through all the bags in the trash can. Yuck!

The smell began to get to her. Ernie went outside.

Kids were playing hopscotch and marbles. Kids were playing red rover and tree tag.

Kids were on the swings. Kids were on the jungle gym.

Marcie was up in the crow's nest again. Ernie wondered if she always played there—on top of everyone else.

Ernie passed by them all. She walked around to the front of the school. There weren't so many kids there.

Then she spotted it—the trash basket by the front door. Of course! The thief wouldn't eat that stuff in the lunchroom. People would see him in the lunchroom. The thief would eat the stolen stuff outside.

Ernie ran to the trash basket.

There wasn't much in it. A few gum wrappers. Some papers. A broken umbrella. Four brown paper bags.

Ernie picked the bags out of the trash. She sat on the ground. She opened each one. She found three apple cores. She found six olives. She found half an egg salad sand-

wich. She found a lot of plastic bags. But no Twinkies wrapper, and no orange peel.

Michael ran past her. "Martians eat garbage!" he yelled.

Ernie stuck out her tongue. "Just you wait!" she yelled after him.

But Michael didn't hear her. He had on his headphones, and he was running too fast, anyway. Ernie watched him disappear off the playground and down the street.

Ernie was in no hurry to get home that afternoon. She needed to think. She thought best when she was walking.

The thief wasn't Dinosaur Don. The thief probably ate outside. Who could it be?

The lunches all started out on Room 123's coat rack. Who went there? The kids in Room 123 mostly. It must be somebody in her class. But who?

Michael. That's who she wanted it to be.

But Michael ate in the lunchroom. And his Twinkie was always missing.

Wait a minute. Maybe it *was* Michael. He could be stealing his own Twinkie. That would make it look like he wasn't the thief. Pretty smart. And where was he running today after lunch? To eat the stolen lunch? Maybe.

Ernie kicked a stone. Poor shoe bear. He looked like he had banged his nose.

Suddenly, she stopped short. Her eagle eye had spotted something. Something orange. It was sticking out of the trash basket just ahead on the corner of Maple and Elm.

Ernie ran to the basket. She dug through the trash.

There—she had it!

It was an orange peel. And right there next to it was a Twinkies wrapper!

"Hooray!" Ernie shouted. She had it all figured out now. It was Michael, all right.

He stole his own Twinkie. He stole the other stuff, too. He ran down here to eat it after lunch. Then he threw his trash in this basket.

Ernie had seen him running this way today. Tomorrow she would catch him in the act!

CHAPTER 5

The Trap

On Thursday morning, Ernie put her lunch at the bottom of her backpack. She wouldn't be eating it in the lunchroom today. She would be eating lunch at the corner of Maple and Elm.

At noon, Ernie put on her jacket. She grabbed her backpack. She hurried outside. She ran down the street. She looked both ways. Then she crossed the street and ran down the hill.

The trash basket was in a good spot. There was a row of tall bushes at that corner. There were trees behind the bushes. Probably there was a house behind the trees, but Ernie couldn't see it.

Ernie crawled under the bushes. She tried to step carefully. Her two white bears were getting messier by the minute. One of them had lost his tail. The other had lost an ear.

She sat down next to a tree. She took her lunch bag out of her backpack. She took an apple out of her lunch bag. She bit into it. *Crunch*.

"Shhh," said Ernie. She had to eat quietly. She wished Mommy had given her a banana instead of an apple.

Ernie chewed as softly as she could. She finished the apple. Then she ate her sandwich. Now there was nothing to do but wait.

Ernie waited.

Mr. Oliver, their mailman, passed by. Then a lady pushing a baby stroller. But no Michael.

An old man dropped a pipe cleaner into the trash basket. A lady dropped in a torn shopping bag. But no one dropped in any Twinkies wrappers.

The lunch walkers were heading back to school. Ernie saw Carmen and Geraldine. They were whispering together and giggling. Ernie hoped they weren't giggling about her.

She saw William.

She saw Jo-Jo go by. He was trying to whistle. It sounded more like wind than whistle.

She didn't see Michael at all.

The warning bell rang. Ernie ran back to school. She hung up her jacket. She took her seat.

Maybe Michael wasn't the lunch bag

thief, or maybe he had quit. Maybe he knew she was on to him.

But the lunch bag thief hadn't quit. He had struck again! Everyone was whispering about it.

When Ms. Finney was called to the office, they stopped whispering. They started talking.

"My Twinkie was missing *again!*" said Michael. "And I know who took it." He looked right at Ernie.

Marcie turned around in her seat. She smiled her sweet, sticky smile. The smell of Juicy Fruit got stronger. Ernie wanted to hold her nose.

"Martian queens are piggies," said Marcie.

"Er-ness-teen is a Martian pig!" sang Michael.

Suddenly, R.T. stood up. "Just stop it, Michael," she said. "I'd rather be a Martian

$$\begin{array}{r} 523 \\ +416 \\ \hline \end{array}$$

than be mean like you." R.T. smiled at Ernie. Then she sat down. She didn't say anything else.

Michael didn't say anything else, either.

When Ms. Finney came back, everyone was studying the spelling list. Everyone but Ernie. She was too busy studying Michael.

He *was* mean. That was why he was doing this. Just to be mean to her.

He must have gone a different way today, Ernie thought. But tomorrow she would be ready for him—no matter which way he went.

Just then something touched her arm. It was William. He handed her a piece of paper.

Ernie turned it over. There was a drawing on the other side. It was a picture of a kitten. White with brown-and-gray spots and a red collar. It looked so real, Ernie thought it might purr.

Ernie looked at him and smiled, but William was studying his spelling list.

On Friday, Ernie had a new plan. She would hide outside all through lunch. Then she would see Michael come out after lunch. She would follow him, wherever he went. She would catch him in the act!

When the lunch bell rang, Ernie put on her jacket. She left her backpack on the shelf. She wouldn't have time to eat her lunch today, so she didn't need her backpack to carry it in.

Ernie stood on the playground. She needed a place to hide. But she had time to find one. Michael wouldn't come out for a while.

Ernie watched the walkers leave. Carmen and Geraldine. William. Jo-Jo. He was still trying to whistle.

Suddenly, her eagle eye noticed something. Carmen and William had their backpacks with them. No one else did.

42

Why would they carry their backpacks home at lunchtime? Ernie could think of only two reasons.

1. They were studying at lunchtime.
2. They were carrying a stolen lunch!

Ernie changed her plan. She didn't wait for Michael. She followed Carmen and William.

Carmen and Geraldine walked down the street together. They looked both ways. Then they held hands and crossed the street.

William walked a ways behind them.

Ernie walked a ways behind William.

At the bottom of the hill, William turned right. Carmen and Geraldine turned left.

Ernie did some quick thinking.

Carmen was very smart. Maybe she studied at lunchtime. Maybe that was why she was so smart.

William didn't like to study. He liked to draw.

Ernie didn't want the lunch bag thief to

be William, but she had to know. She had to follow him, but she had to be careful. She couldn't let him see her.

Ernie stopped at the corner. She gave William time to get halfway down the block. Then she turned the corner.

The street was empty. William had disappeared.

Ernie put her brain to work. Maybe William lived on this block. Maybe he had gone inside his house.

But maybe not. Maybe William was somewhere behind the bushes. Maybe William was hiding today where Ernie had hidden yesterday.

Quietly, Ernie crawled under the bushes again. She peeked around a tree. No William. Ernie tiptoed to the next tree. She peeked around it. Still no William. She tiptoed to the next tree, then the next, then the next. And then she saw him!

He was sitting on his jacket underneath a tree. There was a spot of jelly on his chin. He was eating a peanut butter-and-jelly sandwich. Ernie wondered whose it was today.

CHAPTER 6

The Capture

Ernie didn't tiptoe anymore. She leaped out from behind her tree.

"I got you!" she whooped. Then she swooped down on William. She pinned him to the ground. She didn't want William to be the thief. Now that he was, she was madder than ever.

William started to cry. "Don't beat me

up!" he cried. "Please don't beat me up!"

Ernie sat back. She stared at William.

"I'm not going to beat you up, William," she told him. "I'm just going to take you to Mr. Conway's office."

William cried harder.

Ernie didn't know what to do now. "Cut that out!" she said.

William was wrecking everything. Ernie had caught him, hadn't she? She was supposed to feel good. But she *liked* William. His crying made her feel terrible.

"What did you think was going to happen?" Ernie asked him. "You stole the lunches, didn't you? And look what you did to my shoes. My two white bears are brown bears now."

"I only took one thing from each lunch," William said, sobbing. "Dinosaur Don takes all of mine."

"Every day?" Ernie asked.

William nodded.

"He'll beat me up if I don't give him my lunch," he said.

"Why don't you just tell someone?" asked Ernie.

"He'll beat me up if I do that, too." William sniffed. "I'm sorry about your shoes, Ernie," he said. "Really I am."

"I know you are," said Ernie. "I liked your picture of the kitten."

Ernie felt inside her pocket. She found a Kleenex. She handed it to William.

"It's not dirty," she said. "Just wrinkled. Blow."

William blew.

"What about yesterday?" said Ernie. "You weren't here yesterday."

"I ate in the park yesterday," said William. "Under the bushes."

"Oh," said Ernie. Something was still wrong here. What was it?

"Wait a minute, William," she said. "I saw Dinosaur Don dump his lunch tray.

There was nothing on it. He didn't throw away any lunch bags."

William wiped his eyes.

"That wasn't his tray," he said. "It was Skinny Emily's. He always finishes her lunch. He must have thrown my bag away before."

"What a pig," said Ernie. She thought for a minute. "And that's just how we're going to get him."

"Huh?" said William.

"Listen," said Ernie. "I won't tell on you. Just stop stealing lunches, okay?"

"But what am I going to eat?" asked William.

"Your own lunch," said Ernie. "After Monday, Dinosaur Don will leave you alone."

"He will?" said William.

Just then the warning bell rang.

"Come on," said Ernie. "I'll tell you my plan on the way back to school."

CHAPTER 7

The Big Bad Lunch

On Sunday afternoon, Ernie cleared off her desk. She moved Harold to her bed. She put her crayon case into her top drawer. She put her *Big Book of Dinosaur Masks to Color and Cut Out* into her bottom drawer. She put the picture of her class last year on top of her bookcase. She put Daddy's old giant office calendar under her bed. She spread a newspaper over her desk.

Then she went to the kitchen. She knew exactly what she wanted. She and William had figured it all out on Friday.

2 slices of bread
1 small empty jar
1 bigger jar filled with orange juice
1 carton of plain yogurt
1 bottle of chocolate syrup
1 can of garlic powder
1 bowl
1 knife
1 spoon
1 plastic sandwich bag

Ernie carried everything to her bedroom. She lined it all up on her desk.

When William came over, she was ready. She took him straight to her room.

"Let's see yours," said Ernie.

William put his backpack on her chair. He opened it.

"Here," he said. He handed her a can of

dog food. Then he handed her a can opener. Next came a bottle of hot sauce. Then a plastic bag of carrot sticks and a paper lunch bag. Finally, he pulled out two pieces of lettuce.

"What's that for?" asked Ernie.

"My mom always puts lettuce on my sandwiches," said William.

"Good thinking, William," said Ernie. She slapped him on the back. "We have to make this lunch look just like all the rest."

William grinned. "That's why I brought the carrots, too," he told her.

They got right to work.

William opened the dog food.

Ernie picked up the knife. She spread the dog food on a slice of bread.

"Make it really thick," said William.

Ernie did. William laid the lettuce on top. Ernie put the other slice of bread on top of that. Then they tucked the sandwich into the plastic bag.

"Oh, boy!" said William. "I can't wait till Monday!"

"Me too!" said Ernie.

Next Ernie dumped the yogurt into the bowl. William added some chocolate syrup. They took turns stirring it together.

"It looks like chocolate pudding," said William. He stuck his finger into the bowl. He licked his finger.

"Mmmm," he said. "It's yummy."

"Just wait," said Ernie. She dumped in the garlic powder. William stirred.

"Let's taste it now," said Ernie.

They each stuck a finger into the bowl.

"Ready. Set. Go!" said Ernie.

They both licked their fingers.

"Aargh!" William choked.

"Yuck!" said Ernie.

They ran to the bathroom for a glass of water.

"Just wait till he eats that!" said William.

He began to giggle.

"Yeah," said Ernie. She began to giggle too.

They spooned the pudding into the small jar.

"Now the juice," said Ernie. She opened the bigger jar.

William opened the hot sauce. He poured some into the orange juice.

"More," said Ernie.

William added more.

They stirred it up. Then they screwed the cap back on the jar.

They put the lunch into the lunch bag. They put the lunch bag into William's backpack. They cleaned up. Then they sat on the floor and laughed and laughed.

"Don't forget to put it in the refrigerator tonight," said Ernie. "We want it to smell real good tomorrow morning."

CHAPTER 8

Dinosaur Don

Monday morning, Ernie was worried. When she poured her cereal, she spilled it. When she toasted her bread, she burned it.

"Is something the matter?" Daddy asked.

"I'm just thinking," said Ernie.

"Oh," said Daddy. He turned the page of his newspaper.

Ernie chewed on her toast and thought.

"Can a person die from eating dog food?" she asked.

Daddy put down his paper. "I never heard of anyone dying from dog food," he said.

"I bet a person could get really sick, though," said Ernie.

"Not unless that person ate an awful lot of it," said Daddy.

"A can?" said Ernie.

"More than that," said Daddy. "Ten cans maybe."

"What about from eating garlic powder and hot sauce?"

"Nope," said Daddy. "I've even heard that garlic is good for you."

Ernie felt better.

Ernie step-hopped all the way to school. She sang,

"Who's afraid of the Big Bad Lunch,
The Big Bad Lunch,

The Big Bad Lunch,
Who's afraid of the Big Bad Lunch?
Dinosaur Don, that's who!"

She step-hopped straight to the swings.
William was already there.

"Did he take it?" Ernie asked.

"Yes!" said William. "Do you really think
this will work?"

"Sure it will," said Ernie.

They both started to giggle.

Ernie thought the morning would never
end. Finally, the lunch bell rang.

Ernie was first in line. Michael was right
behind her. Then William. Ernie hopped from
one foot to the other.

"Where's the fire, Ernie?" said Ms.
Finney. "Settle down now."

"Yes, ma'am," said Ernie.

"Martian talk," whispered Michael.

Ernie wished she could fix *his* lunch.

William and Ernie sat next to each other at the lunch table. Ernie shared her lunch with him. She had brought two sandwiches today, and two apples, and two brownies.

R.T. sat across from them.

"Sit on this side with us, R.T.," said Ernie. They could see Dinosaur Don from their side.

"Why?" asked R.T.

"You'll get to see something," Ernie told her.

R.T. pushed her lunch across the table. Then she walked around.

"I don't believe Marcie, Ernie," she said. "I don't think you are the lunch bag thief."

"Marcie?" said Ernie. "It's Michael who says I am the thief."

"Marcie started it," said R.T. "That very first day. Michael just called you a Martian. He calls everyone a Martian sometimes.

Even people he likes."

Ernie smiled at R.T. Maybe they would make a shoe zoo after all. Then she whispered into R.T.'s ear. She told her what was in Dinosaur Don's lunch.

Just then, Dinosaur Don sat down at the fifth-grade table. He opened William's lunch bag. He took out the sandwich. He unwrapped it. He lifted it up. He opened his mouth. Then he closed his mouth. He sniffed the sandwich.

Ernie and William held their breath. R.T. chewed her braid.

Then Dinosaur Don bit. He chewed. He swallowed. He bit again. He chewed. He swallowed. Then he bit again.

Ernie and William and R.T. could hardly stand it.

"He likes it!" said William.

"Dinosaur Don the Dog Face!" said R.T.

All three of them exploded in giggles.

"What's so funny, Martians?" said Michael.

"Should we tell him?" Ernie asked William.

William nodded. He was laughing too hard to talk.

Ernie whispered the secret across the table. Soon the whole class was watching Dinosaur Don.

By now D.D. had finished the sandwich. He pulled the pudding out of the bag. Then he pulled out a spoon.

"Good thinking, William!" said Ernie. She had forgotten all about putting in a spoon for the pudding.

William beamed.

D.D. opened the jar. He spooned up a giant spoonful of pudding. He opened his mouth. He spooned it in.

Suddenly, his face got white. His eyes got big. He grabbed his throat.

Then he grabbed the orange juice. He took a giant swallow.

Crash! Dinosaur Don's chair fell to the floor.

"Aaaaargh!" His mouth opened wide. He ran for the door.

They could hear him yelling all the way down the hall.

CHAPTER 9

The Martians

Room 123's table erupted. Michael and Tommy hollered. Jason whooped right out loud. Sammy laughed so hard his glasses fell right off his nose. Ellen cheered and gave her apple to William. Even Marcie cheered, but not very much.

R.T. cheered the loudest of all. "Neat-o!" she shouted. "Neat-neat-neat-NEAT-O!"

Ernie and William jumped up and down. "It worked!" they cried. "It worked!"

They weren't the only ones cheering.

The secret had passed from one table to the next. When Dinosaur Don drank his orange juice, the whole school knew what was going on. And everyone knew whose lunch it was, too. William was a hero.

Big kids—even sixth-graders—came over to Room 123's table. "Good for you!" they told William. "Way to go!"

"It was Ernie's idea," William told them all.

By the end of the day, they were both stars. Everyone seemed to know that William drew the best pictures. Everyone knew that Ernie was new in school, too— and that she came from Newport News, Virginia, *and* that she had an eagle eye!

Teachers in the halls smiled at William and Ernie. Even Mr. Conway smiled at them. Ernie wished he would do something else.

"Well, Ernie," said Ms. Finney at the end of the day. "This has been quite a week. It looks like you have taken White Bear Lake by storm."

"Yes, ma'am," said Ernie. She felt her cheeks getting warm.

"I've never had a detective in my class before," said Ms. Finney.

"No, ma'am," said Ernie.

Ms. Finney smiled. "Have a good afternoon, dear," she said.

When Ernie left, Ms. Finney was shaking her head, but she was still smiling.

William and R.T. were waiting for her in the hall. William was hopping around R.T. R.T. was hopping around William. Ernie couldn't help but hop, too.

"This is the best day of my life so far!" said William.

"Mine too!" said Ernie.

"This is the best day this school ever

had!" said R.T. "C'mon. Let's go start making that shoe zoo."

The three friends skipped outside onto the playground.

Michael was hanging by his knees on the jungle gym. When he saw them, he jumped off.

"Uh-oh," said William. "What does he want?"

"Who cares?" said Ernie. She linked arms with William and R.T. "We're the Martian queens! And the Martian king," she added.

Michael caught up with them by the swings. He took off his headphones. He hung them around his neck.

"Can I be a Martian king, too?" he asked.

"Well, I don't know," said Ernie. "What do you think, Martians?" She looked at William and R.T.

"Martian kings can't be mean," said R.T.

"I won't be," said Michael.

"You have to be a Martian prince first," said Ernie.

"All right," said Michael.

"And you have to do something to prove you are a Martian," said William.

"I already did," said Michael. He pointed at his feet.

Ernie and R.T. and William looked at his shoes.

Ernie guessed Michael had done them in a hurry. The mouths were crooked. The eyes were lopsided. And they didn't have ears. But they were still bears.

R.T. giggled. "They look like Martian bears!" she said.

"Then he must be a Martian!" said Ernie.

And the four friends skip-hopped down the sidewalk, singing,

"The Martians went over the mountain,
The Martians went over the mountain,
The Martians went over the mountain,
And caught a dinosaur!"

BUY ONE **EAGLE-EYE ERNIE**™ MYSTERY AND RECEIVE ONE FREE!

The adventures continue... but not the cost!

Regulations:

1. All coupons must include proof of EAGLE-EYE ERNIE purchase.
2. Limit one free book per household.
3. Offer expires May 31, 1991
4. Entries must be legible. Not responsible for lost or misdirected mail.
5. Simon & Schuster employees and their families are not eligible.

SEND THIS COMPLETED COUPON
AND PROOF OF PURCHASE TO:

Ken Geist, Marketing Director
Simon & Schuster Children's Books
1230 Avenue of the Americas, New York, New York 10020

I have read the following EAGLE-EYE ERNIE mystery:

#1 _____ EAGLE-EYE ERNIE COMES TO TOWN
#2 _____ THE BOGEYMAN CAPER
#3 _____ THE TAP DANCE MYSTERY
#4 _____ THE CAMPFIRE GHOSTS

Fill in your name and address and soon you will receive your free EAGLE-EYE ERNIE book.

_____
Name

_____
Address

_____
City, State   Zip code